KART
RIVAL

BY JAKE MADDOX

text by
Derek Tellier

STONE ARCH BOOKS
a capstone imprint

Jake Maddox JV Boys books are published by
Stone Arch Books
a Capstone imprint
1710 Roe Crest Drive
North Mankato, Minnesota 56003

www.mycapstone.com

Library of Congress Cataloging-in-Publication Data is available on the Library of
Congress website.

ISBN: 978-1-4965-7523-4 (library hardcover) — 978-1-4965-7526-5 (paperback) —
978-1-4965-7528-9 (ebook PDF)

Summary: When Sheldon spends the day with his aunt, he has no idea he's about to enter
the fast-paced world of kart racing. Sheldon's not one for sports, but the combination of
technical skill and adrenaline, along with an opposing bully, pulls him onto the track. Will
Sheldon cross the finish line first, or will his dreams of kart racing break down?

Editor: Gena Chester
Designer: Sarah Bennett

Photo Credits: Shutterstock: Franck Boston, Design Element, Nicky Rhodes, Cover,
Interior Design Element

Printed and bound in China.
000970

TABLE OF CONTENTS

CHAPTER 1

START YOUR ENGINE

All Sheldon wanted to do was fly his drone, but Aunt Lucy told him to get in the truck. They were going to the speedway.

On the way, Sheldon took his phone out of his pocket. "Nope, put it away," said Aunt Lucy.

Aunt Lucy was his dad's sister. And since Sheldon's dad wasn't around much, neither was she. From what Sheldon could remember, this was the first time they had hung around each other one-on-one.

He'd been riding shotgun for what felt like hours when they drove past the first speedway. "How many speedways do you have around here?" Sheldon asked.

"Plenty," said Aunt Lucy. "That's the Carver County Speedway. We're going to the High Octane Speedway."

"What's the difference?" Sheldon asked.

"The kids at High Octane race like they mean it," said Aunt Lucy.

Sheldon was spending a week at his aunt's place in the country. When she had come into the city to pick him up, Sheldon's mom said, "Remember, Aunt Lucy doesn't beat around the bush." Sheldon decided he liked his aunt's no-nonsense attitude.

As soon as he spotted the High Octane Speedway sign, Sheldon's curiosity grew. The parking lot was packed. There were pick-up trucks everywhere and tons of go-karts on trailers.

Sheldon admired the karts. They weren't what he imagined. When Sheldon pictured a go-kart, he thought of bulky box cars on wheels, usually with bumpers for safety. However, the racing karts at High Octane looked like the small Indy cars he'd seen on TV.

"The racers build those themselves?" asked Sheldon.

"Most of them," said Aunt Lucy.

Sheldon loved to build things. So far, he had built his drone, put together model cars, and assembled some remote-control robots. The idea of adding a racing car to that list appealed to him. His mind started to wander to body styles, colors, and special racing suits.

Aunt Lucy bought him a ticket and led him into the grandstand. Almost no one sat on the bleachers. Most of the crowd stood along the fence of the racetrack. Sheldon and Aunt Lucy joined them and settled in along the fence.

Racing karts took laps around an asphalt oval. To Sheldon, they looked fast, faster than a car on the highway. Aunt Lucy said, "This group's older than you, but not by much."

Sheldon nodded, but he wasn't really paying attention. He was too caught up in the craftsmanship of the karts. They were so sleek that they looked like they'd been made by a professional, not homemade in a garage. Everyone looked just as excited—if not more so—as he was.

"I didn't know this was such a big thing," Sheldon said.

"Bud," said Aunt Lucy, "you gotta get out of that city more."

The racers drove into position at the starting line. Once they situated themselves, everything quieted down. Then a roar filled the track as each driver punched the gas pedal.

Sheldon didn't know what he liked better, the speed or the engineering. The overall effect was hypnotizing. He couldn't imagine anyone would be able to resist its pull. That made him think.

"Did my dad ever come to the speedway?" asked Sheldon.

"Yeah, bud," said Aunt Lucy, "he was a regular."

The karts came around, and each of their colors smeared together. Stickers from the sponsors, racers' helmets, and the karts themselves were all a blur. Everything was new and exciting to Sheldon. From the fresh wave of exhaust smoke that hit him as the karts passed by, to the smell of burned rubber on the track, he was hooked immediately.

"This is cool," he said.

"I thought you'd like it," said Aunt Lucy, "with you into building things."

Two racers nudged their karts against each other. They pushed to the finish. One kart wrestled the other off and speeded to victory.

The winner took a victory lap. Other competitors pulled off the track. Racers from a younger division entered. Aunt Lucy said to Sheldon, "These kids are your age."

A flash of red caught Sheldon's eye. He pointed at the racer. "Who's that?"

"That," said Aunt Lucy, "is Cole Olson. But other racers call him the Coal Roller."

The Coal Roller burned rubber in a black kart with red flames on the sides. His helmet had the same flame design as his kart. A large cloud of black smoke streamed nonstop out of his tailpipe.

Sheldon asked, "Can you have smoke come out of your kart like that?"

"Only at High Octane," said Aunt Lucy. "They're extreme. If you can't run with the big dogs, stay home."

Sheldon watched the racers. To him, it looked like they were concentrating, trying to get a feel for the track. Sheldon noticed the Coal Roller smack himself in the helmet as he raced around. The Coal Roller passed someone. As he went around, he shot smoke in their face.

"He calls that coal rolling," Aunt Lucy said. "Passing someone and shooting smoke in their face. He thinks it's cool."

"Why?" asked Sheldon.

"It's in his blood to be dramatic," said Aunt Lucy. "He's an Olson kid. His aunt Darla has to put on a show just walking through the grocery store." Sheldon didn't see how that explained anything. Aunt Lucy, however, was not offering any more information.

Sheldon could see how the Coal Roller's smoke blowing was a way to get in the zone for the race. But Sheldon still didn't like it. To him it seemed like a dirty trick that took away from the racing.

The drivers took their places to begin the heat. The Coal Roller fell in at the end.

"Why is he last?" asked Sheldon.

"He knows he can beat everyone," said Aunt Lucy, "so he starts in last to rub it in."

The race began. The Coal Roller sped in front of a kart, wedged himself between two others, and busted up the middle. His cloud of smoke trailed behind, coloring a major section of track.

To Sheldon, the Coal Roller's actions seemed like something out of a video game. "Is this guy for real?" he asked.

"I'm afraid he is," said Aunt Lucy.

"I wouldn't race like that," said Sheldon.

The Coal Roller won by at least five kart lengths. His smoke oozed all over the track. It blew out by the fence and coal-rolled everyone watching. Aunt Lucy and Sheldon coughed.

* * *

The next morning, Sheldon and Aunt Lucy headed to the Carver County Speedway. They rented a bright green kart for an hour. It looked nice, but it wasn't as cool as Cole's black and red one. A speedway employee drove the kart out to the track, handed Sheldon a helmet, and walked back to the kart shed.

Sheldon felt nervous. He had never driven before. Luckily, they were at the track early enough that no other drivers were there. At least no one other than Aunt Lucy would see him mess up.

Aunt Lucy motioned for Sheldon to look down in front of the driver's seat. She pointed at the pedals. "The one on the left is the brake," she said. "The one on the right is the gas. You know the gas pedal makes it go, right?"

"Yeah," said Sheldon, "I know that."

"Good," said Aunt Lucy. "You're pretty smart for a city boy. Put on the helmet and climb in."

Sheldon did as he was told.

Aunt Lucy pointed at a lever under the steering wheel. "That's the gear shift," she said.

"You move it up when you want to put it in drive. Then, when you hit the gas, the kart will go. It's an automatic, which means the gears will shift all by themselves."

Sheldon put his foot on the brake. He moved the gear shift up but paused before pressing down on the gas.

"Just go slow. Make sure you get a feel for it," said Aunt Lucy.

Sheldon took his foot off the brake. He tapped the gas, and the kart jerked forward. Sheldon slammed on the brakes.

Aunt Lucy started laughing. "It takes some getting used to," she said.

Sheldon tried again. He jerked the kart forward, but once he got going, the jerkiness stopped. He drove slowly and kept his hands wrapped tightly around the wheel. He felt the engine vibrate the seat. He liked the rumble of the motor.

He gave the kart a little more gas. But when a turn came up, Sheldon slowed down. Then he hit the gas for the straightaway. He looked down at the track and saw how fast the asphalt went by.

As Sheldon approached the spot where Aunt Lucy was standing, he could see her waving her arms. He pulled over.

"When you go around the curve," said Aunt Lucy, "drive into the skid. If the rear of the kart pulls to the right, turn your wheels to the right." Aunt Lucy patted him on the shoulder. "The angles are everything. You don't want to lose speed going into a turn, and you don't want to lose speed if another driver hits you."

Sheldon took off, this time without any jerkiness. He felt more comfortable and pushed down harder on the gas pedal. At the turn, he felt the rear of his kart skidding to the right. He turned his wheels into it, corrected the skid, and sped up through the turn.

At the end of the hour, Sheldon stopped the kart and took off his helmet. He gave Aunt Lucy a high five.

"You did well correcting those skids," Aunt Lucy said. "Bud, you might be a natural."

On the drive back to Aunt Lucy's house, Sheldon asked if they had anything like High Octane in the city.

"Not like High Octane," said Aunt Lucy. "Folks out here like their racing. They take it seriously."

Sheldon sat in silence.

Aunt Lucy asked, "Think you'd like to build a kart?"

Sheldon wanted to, but he didn't know how it would be possible. His mom would never let him. His dad would never have time to help him with it.

"We could build it at my place," Aunt Lucy offered.

Sheldon turned toward her excitedly. He would've hugged her, but she was still driving. Besides, Lucy didn't seem like much of a hugger.

"I do want to race out here," said Sheldon.

"At High Octane?" Aunt Lucy asked.

"I don't like how the Coal Roller treats the other drivers," said Sheldon. "Someone needs to show him that there are other ways to win."

"You don't have to call him Coal Roller," said Aunt Lucy. "His name is Cole Olson."

"Whatever his name is, he's disrespectful," said Sheldon.

Aunt Lucy nodded thoughtfully. "I'd love it if you raced out here," she said. "Your mother will hate the idea."

CHAPTER 2

BUMP IN THE ROAD

Sheldon's stay with Aunt Lucy came to an end, and she drove him back to the city. As she pulled into his driveway, they gave each other a fist bump. "All right, bud," said Aunt Lucy, "let's go convince your mom."

Yes, Sheldon explained, he'd had a great time. No, they didn't get into any trouble. Sheldon's mom, who was folding laundry, asked what they had done.

"Just shucked some corn," Aunt Lucy said, "kind of sat around and said 'aww shucks'."

"Stop with your routine," said his mom.

Sheldon said, "We saw a kart race."

"Like a go-kart race?" his mom asked.

"Technically, yes, but they look more like Indy cars," said Sheldon. "Mom, it's awesome."

"It *is* awesome," said Aunt Lucy.

Sheldon pulled his phone out of his pocket. He said, "I took a video."

"Where do you get a kart like that?" asked his mom.

Sheldon looked at his aunt. "You build them."

"Like your drone?" his mom asked.

"Yes," said Sheldon. "Then you take it out to High Octane."

"What is High Octane?" asked his mom.

"It's where you can race with the big dogs." Sheldon said, echoing Aunt Lucy's earlier words.

"Sheldon, tell her what you want to do," said Aunt Lucy.

"I want to build a kart," Sheldon said.

"You can't build one here," said his mom. She spread her arms to show the cramped space.

"I'll do it at Aunt Lucy's," Sheldon said.

"I'd love to build a kart with Sheldon," added Aunt Lucy.

His mom sighed. "He's got school."

"I can get him after school," said Aunt Lucy. "I'll come here any day of the week."

"I can enter it in the engineering meet," said Sheldon.

"You can enter a drone in the engineering meet," said his mom. "You just want to take it out to that rundown race track."

"It's called High Octane," said Sheldon. "I have to stand up to the bully."

That got his mom's attention. "What bully?" she asked.

"The Coal Roller," said Sheldon.

"A kid named Cole Olson," Aunt Lucy said. "He likes to blow smoke—literally."

His mom stared at Aunt Lucy.

"I'm not saying anything that isn't true," said Aunt Lucy.

His mom picked up the towels she had folded and marched into the bathroom. Sheldon could see that she didn't look happy. Sheldon went in after her. "It's the right thing to do," he said.

"No, it isn't," she said. "You're too good of a student. Why distract yourself from that?"

"Mom," said Sheldon, "I can race karts and still be a good student."

"No," she said. "I'm sorry. This just isn't going to work."

* * *

Sheldon and his buddy Pavel rode their bikes to Comic Book World after school. The new issue of *The Human Claw* was out. Both Sheldon and Pavel wanted to buy it.

Sheldon and Pavel walked by a group of kids they knew from school. The three were making fun of *The Human Claw* comics. Sheldon listened and steamed.

The group's rudeness made Sheldon think of the smoke rolling out of the Coal Roller's exhaust pipe. Both were so unnecessary, and both clouded the two things that Sheldon really liked—comic books and kart racing.

When Sheldon got home, he tried to read his new comic. In the story, villains knocked The Human Claw off his motorcycle. The Human Claw fought them off but had to pursue their leader in a streamlined assault vehicle. The assault vehicle was shaped like a small Indy car. Sheldon pictured himself at the High Octane Speedway in hot pursuit of the Coal Roller.

CHAPTER 3

ON THE RIGHT PATH

After school the next day, Sheldon decided to give his dad a call. "Hey," Sheldon's dad said. "I saw the pictures of you at Lucy's. Looked like you had fun."

"I did," said Sheldon. "Where are you?"

Sheldon had to ask because his dad played guitar. He would tour every few months with a hot country band, but something always went wrong. The tours never lasted. Or someone in charge would get mad and throw his dad out of the band. If that happened, he'd work construction or wrangle horses. One time he even ended up painting houses. Sheldon just never knew.

Sheldon's mom and dad were divorced. And since Sheldon lived with his mom, he often had difficulty keeping track of his dad.

"I'm in Dallas for the week," said his dad. "It's hot."

"Who are you playing with?" asked Sheldon.

"I don't know," said his dad. "We're called the Brian and Macy Band. Except no one in the band is named Brian. No one in the band is named Macy. I don't even know what I'm doing here." He sounded like he wanted to say more but didn't. Finally he asked, "What's up with you?"

Sheldon filled his dad in on his time with Aunt Lucy.

"You know," said his dad, "in the days of yore, I raced out at a track called High Octane."

"That's what I want to do," said Sheldon, "with Aunt Lucy."

"Good choice. Lucy knows her karts," his dad said.

"But Mom won't let me," said Sheldon.

"Well," said his dad. "That's her decision. But want me to talk to her?"

"No," said Sheldon. "I want her to say yes, not ban me for life."

"I do know how to push her buttons," said his dad. "Tell her you'll get good grades."

"I already get good grades," Sheldon said.

"So get better than good grades," said his dad. "Prove to her you can do school and kart racing."

"Hmm," said Sheldon. He had a science test tomorrow. He was pretty sure he'd pass, but there was still time to study.

* * *

The next day after school, Sheldon was putting together a model helicopter. It looked pretty cool.

Plus, it flew by remote control. He had just fired it up when his mom opened the door, which knocked it into the wall.

"Mom!" said Sheldon.

"Don't 'Mom' me," she said.

"You doomed my chopper," said Sheldon.

"I got an email from your teacher," his mom said. "Why do you suppose I got it?"

"I don't know," said Sheldon. He actually didn't. With the extra studying session last night, the test was extremely easy. It was all about mass and acceleration, which when he thought about it, had a lot to do with kart racing.

"You got a hundred percent on your test," said his mom. "The only one in your class to do so! Your teacher was very impressed."

"Great," said Sheldon.

"Look," she said, "I know you've been distracted with kart racing, so I'm really happy to see you can still apply yourself to your studies."

Sheldon picked up his helicopter. No major damage, but the propeller was spinning a little crooked. Sheldon tried to straighten it out. He thought back to what his dad had told him on the phone.

"Mom, I can race karts and be a good student. You know I can. I promise my grades won't slip. Plus, I hardly know Aunt Lucy," said Sheldon. "This would give me a chance to become closer with her. And to Dad."

"It'll take more than that to know your father," she said.

"I know," said Sheldon. "But it's a start."

His mom didn't respond, so Sheldon fixed the propeller and hovered the chopper off the table.

He flew it over by his mom. She grabbed it and set it back down on the table and then gave Sheldon a hug.

"OK, you can race karts," his mom said.

"Yes!" His response was immediate.

"But if you get one bad grade, no more trips to the speedway," she said.

"I'll get straight A's," Sheldon promised.

* * *

Aunt Lucy picked Sheldon up from school the next day. He climbed into the truck and gave Lucy a high five.

"You ready to have some fun?" she asked.

They didn't have time to drive all the way out to the country. Aunt Lucy stopped at a racing shop in the suburbs.

"I'd rather go to the one in Carver County," she said, "but this'll do."

Inside the racing shop, the salesman suggested they buy a four-stroke engine. Aunt Lucy insisted on a two-stroke engine.

"Four-strokes are for amusement parks," she said. "They may be more fuel efficient, but they're less powerful than 2-stroke engines. At High Octane, everyone uses 2-strokes."

Aunt Lucy paid for the engine. It seemed expensive to Sheldon, but he wasn't going to tell her no. She put the engine in the back of her pick-up truck and gave Sheldon a fist bump. "Settle in, bud." She said. "This is the first step. There's a whole lot more before you're ready for High Octane."

Sheldon smiled and shook his head.

CHAPTER 4

THE FIRST STEP

Sheldon split his time between the city and the country.

When he was in the city, he studied, built models, and read comics. Most importantly, he watched a lot of kart racing videos. There were so many on the internet, and a lot of them included tutorials on better driving techniques.

When he was in the country, he measured lumber, fired up Aunt Lucy's table-saw, and cut boards for his kart's frame. Aunt Lucy showed him how to screw the boards together. She had built karts with Sheldon's dad, so she had plenty of advice to give him.

While they worked, she told him a little about growing up with Sheldon's dad. They had gone out to High Octane and competed there when they were younger.

"Your dad was the hot-shot. Me, myself, and I were the pit crew. They didn't like girls racing back then," she said.

"That's not fair!" said Sheldon.

"No, it wasn't." Aunt Lucy laughed. "But I was still able to get out and race a couple times."

That made Sheldon feel a little better. "How did you do?" asked Sheldon.

"Not bad," she said with a shrug. "I was just better at putting karts together."

Sheldon looked at the frame of his kart. There were a pile of parts waiting to be added, but they'd already spent a lot of time in the garage. He was proud of how far along it was.

"I can tell. This this thing looks sweet,"
Sheldon said.

Aunt Lucy shook her head. "It's just a frame."

"I know," said Sheldon. "It still looks sweet."

"We can't get any more done today," said Aunt
Lucy. "Let's get out of here. I'll clean up later."

They drove out to High Octane. The speedway
wasn't holding races, but Aunt Lucy thought
some kids might be out there running laps and
adjusting parts. There were indeed some drivers
out there. One of them was Cole Olson. He sped
around in his black kart with the red flames on the
sides as smoke shot out of his tailpipe.

Aunt Lucy and Sheldon stood along the fence.
They watched the racers burn rubber. Even while
practicing, the Coal Roller would speed in front of
people and blow smoke at them. Sheldon cringed.
"I can't stand that guy's attitude," Sheldon said.

An idea popped into Sheldon's head. "I know
what color I want my kart," he said.

"Let me guess. You want it black and red like Cole's," Aunt Lucy said.

"No," said Sheldon. "I want it white and blue. The opposite of his."

"You're a hard-nosed little dude," said Aunt Lucy. "I kind of like it."

"Someone has to show him how to race with some respect," said Sheldon.

Some of Cole's exhaust smoke drifted in Sheldon and Aunt Lucy's direction. They both coughed and waved their hands to clear it out.

"I want to beat him without the circus act," Sheldon said.

"Bud," said Aunt Lucy, "Cole has won a lot of races with that 'circus act'."

"He's never raced me," said Sheldon. He crossed his arms and glared at the black kart as it raced around the others on the track. A fresh, black wave of exhaust smoke hit each racer that Cole passed.

"I'd worry more about getting your kart put together," said Aunt Lucy, laughing. "And then, practice. Lots and lots of practice. You're going to have a hard time beating Cole without it."

Sheldon nodded his head, but he hadn't really heard her. His eyes were tracking the Coal Roller.

PUTTING IN THE WORK

It had been almost a week since Sheldon talked with Aunt Lucy. He was itching to get back into his kart. It looked great, but there was still a lot to be done. When she finally called that weekend, he answered on the second ring.

"Bud," she said. "They got one in three weeks."

Sheldon didn't know what she meant.

"They got a race," said Aunt Lucy, "at High Octane. Let's get to work."

She picked him up from his house in record time. Soon Sheldon stood in Aunt Lucy's garage. He felt the frame of his kart. Sturdy! He looked around and noticed Aunt Lucy had purchased some new accessories.

Aunt Lucy had bought tires, four to put on the kart and four to have as extras. She had engine mounts laying on the tool bench.

From what he'd learned from Aunt Lucy, the engine mounts were important. They kept the engine held tightly to the frame. There was a hydraulic jack for picking up parts too heavy to lift. She'd bought rods for adding extra durability to the kart. She even had the pins to connect the rods. All of the tools were a little overwhelming, but Sheldon was too excited to admit that.

"I'll build it," said Sheldon.

"I know," said Aunt Lucy. "I'll see to it." She pulled a tarp off a pile of even more gear.

Sheldon raised his eyebrows. Under the tarp

was his kart's exterior body panels. One problem. The parts were not white and blue. They were gray.

"Yeah," said Aunt Lucy. "We got to paint 'em and put 'em on."

She left the garage and went into her house. A moment later, she came back in with a box surrounded in duct tape. Sheldon took a box cutter off of Aunt Lucy's workbench and sliced it open.

Inside there were plenty of packing peanuts. From deep within the box, Sheldon withdrew a racing helmet. The helmet was white. It was not white and blue. Sheldon said, "Let me guess, I have to paint this, too?"

"If you don't do it yourself," said Aunt Lucy, "you don't race at High Octane."

"Can I tell you something?" Sheldon asked.

Aunt Lucy nodded.

"I'm awful at painting," he said.

"I can show you," said Aunt Lucy.

"Is there anything you don't know?" Sheldon asked.

"I know a thing or two about a thing or two," she replied.

Sheldon screwed on a tire mount. If one was too loose, a tire could fall off or the kart could go lopsided.

Sheldon tightened the screw as hard as he could and tested the stability of the mount. It felt solid. He fitted a tire and gave it a good spin. When he looked over his shoulder at Aunt Lucy, he saw her nod her approval.

Sheldon felt her looking on as he fastened the other three tire mounts. He worked on them as carefully as he did the first. He knew that if he rushed it, she would say something.

After that, Sheldon put together the side panel brackets. The side panel brackets weren't as important as the tire mounts, but they helped the kart create its body shape—which in turn made the racing vehicle look good. The side panels, along with the front panel, would give the kart its Indy car appearance.

Sheldon thought about Cole Olson's kart. While he didn't want to copy Cole's racing style, the other driver did have a flair for kart design. It was important to Sheldon to make his kart look just as sharp.

Aunt Lucy showed him where to put the engine mounts—toward the back, just in front of the rear tires. They held the engine to the kart.

She made sure Sheldon knew the mounts were very important. But he felt it probably wasn't needed. Sheldon was already fascinated with building things. To him, everything was important. Sheldon secured them exactly where Aunt Lucy told him and tightened them as hard as he could.

Aunt Lucy wrapped two chains around the kart's engine. She stuck the arm of the hydraulic jack under the chains. But that was all she did. Sheldon was excited to learn that she wanted him to run the jack—under her careful supervision of course.

He hit the button to raise the jack's arm. The jack moved the engine into the air. Sheldon positioned the engine above the mounts.

"This part's pretty cool," Aunt Lucy said. "Once you get the engine in, it's a real kart."

Building the kart with Aunt Lucy was really an experience. He could tell she respected every tool and part. She treated each and every thing carefully.

Sheldon could see her excitement when everything came together. Sheldon felt that same excitement in himself. As much as he felt out of place on that first trip into the country with his aunt, right now, he felt at home.

Sheldon carefully lowered the engine onto the mounts. He connected it and screwed it down.

He and Aunt Lucy admired their work. "Looks like a gray Indy car," said Sheldon.

"It sure does," said Aunt Lucy. "We're on the right track."

* * *

The next morning, they loaded the kart onto a trailer and got in Aunt Lucy's pick-up. Pretty soon they were on their way to Carver County Speedway. Sheldon had wanted to go to High Octane, but Aunt Lucy had said he wasn't quite ready for the big dogs yet.

This time, a few other drivers were at the Carver speedway. Not a big audience. He wasn't sure if that was good or bad yet. Sheldon put on his helmet and pulled onto the track.

His new kart had some giddy-up. In fact, Sheldon felt a little nervous with it. He accelerated but then tapped the brakes. The kart sped up and slowed down quickly. Once he got a feel for his machine, Sheldon hit the gas and enjoyed the ride. He loved the sound of the engine. It reminded him of that first day at High Octane.

Sheldon smiled for an entire lap. He picked up speed, skidded around a corner, and regained control. He cruised down a straightaway and weaved to the left and right, just to see how the kart handled, and it handled well. Sheldon felt like he had been driving for years.

After a few more laps, he slowed down and pulled off the track before stopping near Aunt Lucy. Driving those laps felt great. Sheldon wasn't perfect yet, but he knew he could get there. He got out and gave his aunt a high five.

Back at Aunt Lucy's, it was time to paint. They took off the side panels. If they left them on while they painted, paint would splatter all over the engine, the seat, the steering wheel—it would make a mess of the entire kart.

Sheldon sprayed a base layer of white paint over the gray panels.

Next came the tricky part. The blue flames. Aunt Lucy helped him trace the design. "All you got to do now," she said, "is color in the lines."

Sheldon colored in the lines. Well, he painted in the lines, and the kart started looking sharp! The paint Aunt Lucy had purchased was extra glossy. Those blue flames shined!

"You put in a good day's work," said Aunt Lucy. "You positive you are your dad's kid?"

Sheldon laughed. "You sound like Mom."

"That's kind of scary," said Aunt Lucy. "That's actually *really* scary."

* * *

That night, Sheldon fell asleep without trying. He slipped into dreamland and veered off into a nightmare. He drove his white and blue kart. But he quickly spun out of control. Cars rushed by, not karts. Sheldon could tell he was on a highway—a busy one. It was dark. Smoke filled the air.

In the dream, someone pursued him. Sheldon thought it was the Coal Roller, but he couldn't really tell who it was. Sheldon knew a person was driving the kart, and he knew he was afraid of whoever it was.

Sheldon gained control of his kart and raced down the highway. He wove between cars. The enemy pursued. The road curved to the left. Boulders rolled down a hill. They almost hit Sheldon's kart as they spilled onto the road.

Still, the enemy gave chase. The highway came to a bridge. Sheldon gunned it across.

Something was wrong with the engine. Smoke poured out. Sheldon's kart died and rolled to a stop. The other kart pulled in behind Sheldon and nudged his bumper. The kart was gray. The driver got out and took off his helmet.

The other driver was himself.

He sat up in bed and took a deep breath. He had been chasing himself. As much as he tried, Sheldon could not fall back asleep.

CHAPTER 6

READY, SET, RACE!

Aunt Lucy fetched Sheldon from the city every weekend and most days after school. Then Sheldon ran laps at the Carver County Speedway. This was the routine. At least it was until . . .

The Highway Octane Speedway! Sheldon's time had come to face the Coal Roller.

They arrived early. But a lot of folks and their karts were already there. Aunt Lucy and Sheldon hauled theirs right up to the racers' entrance. As they wheeled the kart of the trailer's ramp, the new paint gleamed in the sunlight.

Aunt Lucy moved the truck out of the way. They checked in at the registration booth and made it official.

"Want to call your dad?' Aunt Lucy asked.

"I already left him a voicemail," said Sheldon.

Aunt Lucy nodded. "Let's go fire up our engine." The engines roared to life. "Sounds like racing," she said, shouting over the noise.

Sheldon smiled. Then, he saw a black pick-up pull up to the racers' entrance. Trailing behind it was a black kart with red flames on the sides.

"The Coal Roller," said Aunt Lucy. "Hope you're ready to race like you mean it."

"I am," Sheldon said. "That guy doesn't scare me one bit."

"He's a heck of a racer," said Aunt Lucy. "You know, even without the coal rolling. He's still good behind the wheel."

Sheldon didn't know what Aunt Lucy was trying to get at. But it didn't matter. He could accept it if Cole beat him on talent alone. But he shouldn't have to coal roll other drivers to win a race. That belief was what fueled Sheldon's desire to beat him.

"If I didn't want to race with the big dogs," said Sheldon, "I should've stayed home." He and Aunt Lucy gave each other a fist bump.

"I got something for you." Aunt Lucy jogged back to the truck and pulled a large shopping bag out from under the seat. She offered the bag to Sheldon.

He looked inside. Yes! He took out a white and blue racing suit. Sheldon loved it. He thought it looked like a superhero costume.

It was made of soft leather—strong enough to protect him in a crash but flexible enough to move with him while he raced. He tried to give Aunt Lucy a hug.

"I don't need a hug," said Aunt Lucy. "That look on your face was enough."

Sheldon put on the racing suit. He fastened his helmet. Wearing the uniform focused his thoughts.

The heats began. He didn't race until the third heat, so he had a while. Sheldon tried to have a quiet moment. But that was not easy at a Speedway. The engine sounds and crowds closed in on him.

He moved his kart off to the side and closed his eyes. Sheldon focused. He let the sound of roaring engines fill his mind and clear his thoughts.

Sheldon concentrated on breathing deep, slow breaths. Then he visualized being the first kart across the finish line.

I'm ready, he told himself.

The racers for Sheldon's heat were called. Aunt Lucy gave him a final wave.

"Drive fast," she called.

Sheldon was new at High Octane, so he had

start in the back. The Coal Roller pulled up next to him. Cole flipped up the visor on his helmet. He stared at Sheldon for a second.

Sheldon could tell Cole was sizing him up. The Coal Roller flipped his visor back down just in time for the green light, which meant the race was beginning.

At first, everyone bunched together. Then things loosened up. Space in front of Sheldon became available. The Coal Roller moved quickly to fill the gap. He waved at Sheldon as he passed him. Then the smoke hit.

Sheldon could not see anything other than oily darkness. He could hardly breathe. He coughed. He sped up, but the smoke was still there. It was overwhelming. When he felt himself start to panic, Sheldon decided to lay back a bit and let Cole's exhaust clear out.

Once Sheldon could see, he accelerated again. He gained on the pack. He could see Cole hanging in the middle, toying with some other drivers. Sheldon broke to the outside and gunned it.

He passed a few racers, moving up to third place. He was just ahead of Cole's black-and-red kart. Sheldon moved to the inside. The move blocked Cole from getting in front of him and blinding him.

As far as his positioning went, it felt right. He needed to stay in front of the Coal Roller, at least so he could see without smoke blinding him. From there he could sort out his next move to take the lead.

Someone smashed into Sheldon's rear bumper. Sheldon didn't turn to see who it was. Instead, he slammed on his brakes and held his breath. He didn't know what else to do.

Sheldon felt his kart getting pushed sideways. He remembered Aunt Lucy's advice about correcting skids, so he cranked his wheels and hit the gas. He refocused his mind and held his course.

The pack completed a lap without any more position changes. Sheldon didn't know if he should try to move up or just keep Cole behind him. Before he could decide, he felt another nudge on his rear bumper. Then he saw the Coal Roller move up beside him.

Cole waved at Sheldon for the second time during the race and hit the gas. Once again, Sheldon could see nothing other than the black smoke coming from Cole's tailpipe.

If he slowed down, he would lose his position in the pack of other drivers. But if he accelerated, he might hit another racer or crash into the wall. Sheldon took a chance and gunned the kart as fast as it would go.

When the smoke disappeared, Sheldon found himself even with Cole, who tried to nudge Sheldon off course. Sheldon saw the push coming and steered into it. The karts knocked off each other and stayed even.

The front of Sheldon's kart ran a few inches ahead of Cole's black-and-red kart. Sheldon thought if he gave Cole a nudge, he could move in front of him. He could then focus on the first- and second-place drivers.

Sheldon turned the wheel and gave the Coal Roller a shove. But he had bad positioning. When their karts made contact, Sheldon's got pushed to the outside.

The Coal Roller moved ahead of Sheldon. Once again, Cole's exhaust smoke killed Sheldon's vision.

Sheldon cranked his steering wheel to regain control. He swerved back to the inside where he thought he might find open space.

This time, when the smoke cleared, it was because the Coal Roller had moved up the line. In fact, Sheldon saw that Cole had moved into second place. He was gaining on the leader, and they were coming into the final lap.

Sheldon tried veering to the outside to pass the racer in front of him. The other driver wouldn't let Sheldon get all the way around.

The two of them fought for position until the finish line. In the end, the Coal Roller won, and Sheldon took fourth.

CHAPTER 7

KART RACING SCIENCE

After the race, Sheldon pulled off the track. He found Aunt Lucy and brought his white-and-blue vehicle to a stop. Sheldon got out and pulled off his helmet. "I can do better than that."

"You weren't going to win." Aunt Lucy shook her head. "Not your first time. I thought you ran a gutsy race."

"I didn't come for a participation trophy," said Sheldon. "I can get that at the engineering meet."

"Bud, no one's giving you a trophy," said Aunt Lucy.

Sheldon watched Cole speed around for a victory lap. Sheldon pointed at Cole's black and red kart. "What does he have in that thing," asked Sheldon, "rocket fuel?"

"Knowing the Olson's," said Aunt Lucy, "it could be."

What did I get myself into? he wondered. He and Aunt Lucy decided to stay and watch the next heat for a bit. Before long, the Coal Roller drove up to them.

Cole stopped and took off his helmet. "I like your paint job," he said to Sheldon. "Your helmet's pretty snazzy too."

"Do you watch the races," asked Sheldon, "or just toss out fake compliments?" This was not Sheldon's best moment. But he was still upset about the loss, and Cole didn't seem very genuine.

"My compliments aren't fake," said Cole.

"Everything about you is fake," said Sheldon. "You aren't a legit racer."

"Well, I beat you," said Cole. Sheldon could tell Cole was getting mad. He was glaring at Sheldon. Sheldon did not, however, think Cole was quite as angry as he was.

"You're a circus," said Sheldon.

"Sure, city boy." Cole said while he backed away. "After all, I sure do love to blow smoke." To prove his point, Cole peeled out and threw a big cloud of exhaust smoke their way.

Sheldon and Aunt Lucy swatted it away from their faces. "So," said Aunt Lucy, "that went well."

* * *

The next time Sheldon was at Aunt Lucy's, she told him she had a surprise. When Sheldon walked into her garage, he found another kart parked next to his. The other kart wasn't painted, but it looked ready to race. "That one's mine," said Aunt Lucy. "I built it over the last couple days."

"Why?" asked Sheldon.

"Bud, you can drive, but you don't know anything about karts knocking you around." Aunt Lucy crossed her arms. "I'm gonna knock you around."

They took their karts out to the Carver County Speedway, which was open for practice laps. They took a few warm up laps before banging into each other. No matter what Sheldon did, he couldn't push Aunt Lucy out of the way. They pulled over.

"It's all about leverage," she said. "You can't just nudge your nose over and stop someone. You'll get knocked off course."

They sprang back into action. Sheldon thought about Aunt Lucy's advice. Jockeying for position was all about mass, and acceleration. He'd studied those terms in physical science. He just had to apply them while he was on the track.

Sheldon ran even with Aunt Lucy. She stuttered for just a second, and Sheldon stuck her in the side panel. Her kart skidded off to the side. She gained control and gave Sheldon a thumbs-up.

When Aunt Lucy pulled into Sheldon's driveway, Sheldon was still thinking about his poor performance in the race and on the track that day. He thought his aunt could tell something was bothering him. When he was about to leave the car, she said, "I had fun knocking you around today."

Sheldon shook his head. "It took me long enough to figure out how to drive," he said.

"What's that supposed to mean?" Aunt Lucy asked.

"I should've figured out positioning and leverage before my race. Not after. I'm supposed to be smart, and I can't even figure that out?" The words came out of Sheldon's mouth fast and sharp. There was a long silence. He could feel Aunt Lucy looking at him, but he refused to move his eyes from the truck's dash.

"You know, bud," she said, "racing can be a lonely sport. There's nothing in the kart except for you and your thoughts. Sometimes, those thoughts can be real mean. Sometimes, your biggest opponent is yourself. Know what I'm saying?"

Sheldon thought back to his dream. He had expected Cole Olson to be the one chasing him. But that's not who was behind the wheel. Maybe his biggest enemy was himself.

"You're saying I shouldn't be so hard on myself," he responded. He finally looked over at her.

"Exactly," Aunt Lucy agreed.

"Thank you," he said quietly. "For everything. You're the only one on Dad's side who'll give me the time of day."

Aunt Lucy shook her head. "What about your dad?" she asked.

"He doesn't always give me the time of day," said Sheldon.

"He doesn't always give me the time of day, either," she said. "He's not a bad person. It's just who he is."

The more Sheldon thought about what Aunt Lucy had said about racing, the more it made sense. Cole had more experience than him. Along with coal rolling, that gave him an advantage. And that was something Sheldon had to fix.

CHAPTER 8

LOSING CONTROL

After school the next day, Sheldon studied some kart racing videos. He looked at how the karts bumped into each other. Usually, the winning drivers were the ones who took the best angles.

As he watched, Sheldon received a text. He hoped it was his dad. He hadn't heard from him since before his last race. The more time Sheldon spent with Aunt Lucy, the more he realized how much he missed his dad. But the message was from Pavel.

He wrote: *Want to come over and play video games?*

Not today, wrote Sheldon. *I'm watching kart races.*

Cool, wrote Pavel. *Thought I'd check.*

Sheldon was still studying angles when his aunt called.

"Hey," Aunt Lucy said, "think you're ready for another go?"

Sheldon thought about it before answering. His last race didn't end as well as he hoped it would. When he faced the Coal Roller next, he wanted to make sure he was ready.

"When?" asked Sheldon.

"Two weeks. And I gotta tell you, bud. There's a lot of buzz about the city kid around town. People are pretty impressed with how far you've come in such a short amount of time. Could give Cole some serious competition," she said.

"Do you think my dad will come?" he asked.

"I tried calling him earlier, but there was no

answer," she said after a small pause. "But I left him a voicemail, so we'll see."

"Yeah, sure," Sheldon said. He tried not to sound hurt and started focusing on the upcoming race. "I'm in."

* * *

The time came for Sheldon to race again. He had just started his engine when Cole rolled up next to him.

"That blue and white is awfully pretty!" Cole yelled. "It might turn gray after I coal roll it!" Cole spun his tires and took off. He shot exhaust out at Sheldon and Aunt Lucy.

They didn't make Sheldon start in last this time, but he was still one of the final karts. He looked back. Cole held his position at the end. Sheldon thumped himself in the helmet and gripped the steering wheel as hard as he could.

Green light!

Sheldon found an angle on a driver and knocked him out of the way. Immediately, someone else ran into him, but Sheldon held his ground. Sheldon hit the brakes and then accelerated. The stutter gave him a better angle on the other driver. Sheldon knocked him out of the way and moved up.

He had a few kart-lengths between him and the racers ahead. Sheldon gunned it for the outside and fell into third place.

That was when his mind began to mess with him. *Third place?* Sheldon knew during the last race he couldn't get out of third and eventually fell to fourth. Plus, the Coal Roller was probably gaining from behind.

Sheldon kept gunning. He caught up to the racer in second place. They bumped into each other, but neither could knock the other off course. Sheldon had to lay off the gas a bit to hold his position.

Then, Sheldon thought he smelled something oily. He thought he heard the Coal Roller's engine roaring.

The Coal Roller stormed in front of Sheldon and the other driver. Luckily, the wind blew most of the exhaust out of their way. They didn't get blinded, but Sheldon panicked. He wanted to catch Cole, so he sped up again.

It was a mistake. The move gave the other driver a better angle, who then knocked Sheldon out of the way.

Sheldon regained control. He was in fourth. The driver who had just bumped him was in third. Cole and the lead racer were jockeying for first.

At this point, Sheldon didn't know what to do. He sped up, but it wasn't enough. Once again, Sheldon finished the race in fourth.

CHAPTER 9

PRACTICE MAKES PERFECT

Aunt Lucy drove Sheldon back into the city. She kept telling him he did a nice job, but Sheldon wasn't having it.

"You ran a better all-around race than last time," she said.

"I knew I shouldn't have gunned it," he said. "I did it anyway. I just flipped out."

"You'll figure it out," Aunt Lucy said.

They pulled into Sheldon's driveway. Aunt Lucy rolled down her window. "I know you don't like participation trophies, but I like how you race.

Most newcomers finish in the back of the pack. But you got fourth. You have talent and good instincts. When you started that race, you had confidence. The only other thing you need is experience."

"And Cole Olson has smoke," Sheldon said. He smiled, expecting his aunt to join in on the joke, but Aunt Lucy was not laughing.

"Cole Olson does not win races on dirty tricks alone. He's got talent, instincts, experience, and confidence. Maybe a bit too much confidence, but he's still a good driver. He earned his win today." At her words, Sheldon sunk into his seat. Lucy kept her eye contact. "But, bud, you're gonna earn the next one. I know it." Finally, she smiled.

Sheldon gave Aunt Lucy a high five.

Inside the house, Sheldon's mom wanted to know what had happened.

"I blew it," said Sheldon. "Coal Roller won."

His mom shook her head. "Can I come to the next race?" she asked.

"Are you worried?" asked Sheldon.

"No," said his mom. "I want to see you race."

Sheldon stood there and nodded his head. Kart racing was definitely cool, but man, it was challenging.

The days until the next race passed by. He practiced racing against Aunt Lucy. Out at the Carver County Speedway, they slammed into each other. Sheldon worked on angles and how his kart hugged the turns. With every lap, he felt more confident, more experienced.

One day, as Sheldon and Aunt Lucy drove practice laps, Sheldon saw the Coal Roller pull up on a four-wheeler. He went right up to the fence and watched Sheldon and Aunt Lucy. Sheldon felt like he was being sized up. He tried not to let it bother him, but he did add it to his long list of reasons for wanting to beat Cole.

The practice laps weren't going well. Aunt Lucy had pushed his kart into the infield multiple times. Sheldon kept trying to get the outside position on his aunt and nudge her off the track. But he couldn't get the angle right.

His front bumper, he thought, was two or three inches ahead of where it should have been. When he smashed into Aunt Lucy's side panel, he just couldn't send her speeding into the infield.

Aunt Lucy tapped her brakes and turned her kart into Sheldon's. He lost control and veered toward the outside wall. He turned his wheels to correct, but Aunt Lucy was there to push him into the wall. Sheldon smacked his fists on the wheel.

"Bud," Aunt Lucy said, "I'm just doing it 'cause I love you."

Later, in Aunt Lucy's garage, Sheldon used an impact wrench to tighten some side mounts. When a bolt got tight enough, the impact wrench would shake the entire kart.

He finally turned to Aunt Lucy. He said, "Is all this even worth it?"

"You don't want to kart race anymore?" Aunt Lucy asked.

"No, I do. But it's not going to change anything," Sheldon said. "Cole's still going to coal roll. Maybe it's not even that big of a deal."

Aunt Lucy picked up an electric drill off her workbench. "Answer me this," she said. "Do you like racing karts?"

Sheldon thought about the first day Aunt Lucy brought him to High Octane. He remembered what it felt like driving his kart for the first time. "I love it," he said.

"Then nothing else should matter. You're not going to change the world with just one race, bud. But you can lead by example. Show Cole Olson that there are other ways to win." Aunt Lucy went back to greasing a spark plug. "Sooner or later, he might get the message."

CHAPTER 10

THIRD TIME'S THE CHARM

Sheldon wheeled his kart off the trailer and headed in through the racers' entrance. He saw Mom and Pavel standing along the fence. They looked nervous. They kept looking out at the track and then looking down at their phones. Sheldon hoped they would settle down and enjoy the race. He was nervous enough as it was—he didn't need their nerves adding to his.

Sheldon started his engine. As usual, the Coal Roller pulled up in a black pick-up. Sheldon watched Cole unload his kart.

Cole pulled up to Sheldon and Aunt Lucy. He said, "You can't practice enough to beat me." He then peeled out and blew exhaust smoke at them.

Aunt Lucy and Sheldon wafted smoke out of their faces.

"Today is the day," said Aunt Lucy. Sheldon didn't say anything. He wanted to beat the Coal Roller, more now than ever, but he didn't know if he could.

Aunt Lucy sensed Sheldon's nerves. "Go out and run your race," she said. "There's nothing else you can do."

After some warm-up laps, Sheldon and Aunt Lucy watched other racers do their thing. Finally, the announcer called for Sheldon's heat.

Sheldon got to start in the middle of the pack. He turned around. He saw Cole fall in at the end. Cole flipped up his visor and yelled something. Sheldon couldn't tell what is was, but he figured it was something like, *The blue-and-white kart's going down.* Cole flipped his visor back down and got ready to begin the race.

Green light!

The racers bunched together. They bumped. Some drivers got knocked out of the way.

Sheldon slid into the middle. He wanted the inside instead of the outside. He'd noticed in his past races that the outside had been slowing him down. Sheldon slammed up against another driver and shoved him out of the way. Sheldon arrived on the inside of the track.

A driver from the outside bumped up against him and tried to shove. If Sheldon screwed up, he would end up in the infield grass. Sheldon held his position and waited for an angle. He tapped his brakes, accelerated, and shoved. He nudged the kid off course and sped ahead.

Two kids ran ahead of Sheldon. He wanted to get in front of them before the Coal Roller made his push.

Too late. Sheldon heard a familiar, irritating engine coming up behind him. He smelled oily smoke. The Coal Roller was here.

Cole roared into the lead. How he weaved in between the people ahead of him, Sheldon had no idea. Maybe Aunt Lucy was right. Maybe there actually was talent behind all that smoke.

Just as Sheldon thought this, Cole's exhaust smoke threw one of the lead racers off course. Sheldon moved into third.

Cole toyed with the second-place driver. He nudged him out of the way and blew exhaust at him. The kid in second veered off. Sheldon took his place.

Cole's and Sheldon's karts jockeyed for first. Sheldon knew Cole was messing with him. He had to be smart. If Sheldon made any mistakes, he would lose. Again.

Sheldon held position on the inside of the track. Cole tried to push him into the infield.

Sheldon watched the angles and held his position. They bumped into each other, each one looking for an opportunity.

Sheldon noticed Cole kept trying to push him into the infield. Cole was toying with him. Sheldon wondered what would happen if, at the right moment, he slammed on his brakes. If Cole tried to nudge and missed, Sheldon could veer to the right, gun it, and push Cole off the track. The angles would be right.

Cole kept trying to nudge him. To Sheldon, it seemed like Cole was being too aggressive and too confident.

Cole's final move was coming. Sheldon knew it. He smelled the Coal Roller's exhaust and heard the rev of its engine. . . .

Sheldon hit his brakes. Cole tried to wrestle his kart against Sheldon's, but Sheldon was behind him. Sheldon accelerated and pushed the front of his kart against the back of Cole's.

The angle he took for the push was perfect.

The Coal Roller spiraled off into the infield. Sheldon looked back. He saw Cole pounding his hands against his steering wheel. The wind caught Cole's exhaust smoke and blew it right back on him.

Sheldon gunned it. All the way to the finish line. He won.

He did not take a victory lap. He drove his kart over to where Aunt Lucy was standing, took off his helmet, and hugged her. She picked him up and whirled him around.

"Bud, I am so proud of you," she said.

His mom and Pavel made their way over to him.

"Congratulations, Sheldon!" his mom said.

Pavel gave him a serious fist bump.

"I have a surprise for you," said Aunt Lucy, pointing behind her.

Sheldon's dad marched through the entrance.

"If I told you he was here," said Aunt Lucy, "you would have lost focus."

All of Sheldon's crew joined in for a hug. They congratulated Sheldon. He was enjoying his victory when Cole pulled up in his kart. Sheldon got ready for some bad-mouthing.

None came.

"Nice job," Cole said. "I think we'll have some good races in the future." Cole held out his hand.

"I think we will too," said Sheldon, holding back his surprise. "To the future." Sheldon walked over and shook Cole's hand.

Cole waved and drove off without coal rolling them. Maybe he wasn't so bad after all.

CHAPTER 11

NEW BEGINNINGS

Aunt Lucy had a million parts laying around. She had so many, it looked like she was starting her own shop.

"I have a plan," said Aunt Lucy. "We're going to build karts. We'll build them. We'll sell them. We'll laugh all the way to the bank."

"I'm a little confused," said Sheldon.

"We might not laugh all the way to the bank," said Aunt Lucy, "but we can make a few bucks while we hang out."

Sheldon was still confused.

"A bunch of drivers called," she said. "They want your kart." Aunt Lucy laughed. "I said we could build them their own, and they said fine."

"I don't know," said Sheldon.

"I'll buy the parts and make sales," said Aunt Lucy. "You build the karts. We'll start a family business."

Sheldon thought about how cool it would be to build more karts with Aunt Lucy. "If Dad leaves another band," he said, "do you think he can help us?"

"Sure," said Aunt Lucy, "if he wants to."

Sheldon asked, "What if one of our karts beats our own?"

"Bud, there is no way anyone is beating you on that track. Especially not with all the extra practice laps you're putting in with Cole," said Aunt Lucy.

Sheldon smiled. He started kart racing thinking he would be facing the ultimate enemy. But as it turned out, enemies were for comic books.

Sheldon and Cole were more like rivals. He could even see them being friends one day.

Sheldon looked over at his aunt. If he did build karts, he would spend more time with Aunt Lucy. *Yes!* Sheldon gave Aunt Lucy a fist bump, picked up a board, and fired up the table saw. He had work to do.

ABOUT the AUTHOR

Derek Tellier is the author of six children's books, including two others in the Jake Maddox series. His poetry and short fiction have appeared in *Secret Laboratory*, *New Verse News*, *Ascent Aspirations*, and numerous other literary journals. He holds a Master of Fine Arts degree in Creative Writing from Minnesota State University, Mankato. He is a writer, teacher, and musician in the Twin Cities in Minnesota.

GLOSSARY

acceleration (ak-sel-uh-RAY-shuhn)—the increase of speed of a moving object

asphalt (AS-fawlt)—a black tar that is mixed with sand and gravel to make paved roads

exhaust (eg-ZAWST)—the waste gases that come out of a car

gear (GEER)—a toothed wheel that fits into another toothed wheel

legit (LEJ-it)—slang for legitimate; real or lawful

leverage (LEV-ur-ej)—the action of gaining an advantage

mass (MASS)—the amount of material in an object

pedal (PED-uhl)—a lever on a kart that riders push with their feet

tailpipe (tayl-PIPE)—an a metal pipe in which exhaust leaves the kart

velocity (vuh-LOSS-uh-tee)—the speed and direction of a moving object

DISCUSSION QUESTIONS

1. In his dream, the driver chasing Sheldon is . . . Sheldon. Why do you think this is?

2. Reread the pages 62–63. Do you think Sheldon should've treated Cole this way?

3. List three things you like about Sheldon. Use examples from the story to support your answers.

WRITING PROMPTS

1. Sheldon loses confidence in himself as racer because he didn't beat Cole Olson. Write about a time when you've lost confidence in yourself. How does it compare to Sheldon's experience?

2. Pretend you are Sheldon. Write a letter to your dad asking him to come home.

3. Write a scene where Cole and Sheldon practice racing with each other. How is their behavior similar to the beginning of the story? How is it different?

MORE ABOUT KART RACING

Danika Patrick, Michael Schumacher, Tony Stewart, and Sarah Fisher all raced karts before having successful careers in professional racing.

International Kart Federation (IKF) and World Karting Association (WKA) are both governing bodies for karting in the United States. The Motor Sports Association (MSA) is the governing body in the UK.

2-stroke engines are lighter than their 4-stroke counterparts. They're also louder and make the common buzzing engine sound heard at most speedways.

Some karts can go faster than 100 miles per hour (160 kilometers per hour).